THIS BOOK BELONGS TO

- - - - - - - - - - - - - - - - - -

For Leo and Jules xx – L.C.

For Ciaran, Owen and Noah x – N.D.

IMPORTANT INFORMATION:
DO NOT EAT! →

ORCHARD BOOKS
First published in Great Britain in 2022 by Hodder & Stoughton
2 4 6 8 10 9 7 5 3 1

Text © Lou Carter, 2022 • Illustrations © Nikki Dyson, 2022
The moral rights of the author and illustrator have been asserted.
All rights reserved. A CIP catalogue record for this book
is available from the British Library.

ISBN 978 1 40836 513 7
Printed and bound in China

Orchard Books, an imprint of Hachette Children's Group
Part of Hodder & Stoughton
Carmelite House, 50 Victoria Embankment
London EC4Y 0DZ

An Hachette UK Company
www.hachette.co.uk

www.hachettechildrens.co.uk

OSCAR

the Hungry Unicorn

AND THE NEW BABYCORN

Lou Carter Nikki Dyson

ORCHARD

Oola has a new baby unicorn!
She absolutely cannot **WAIT**
to welcome her into the palace...

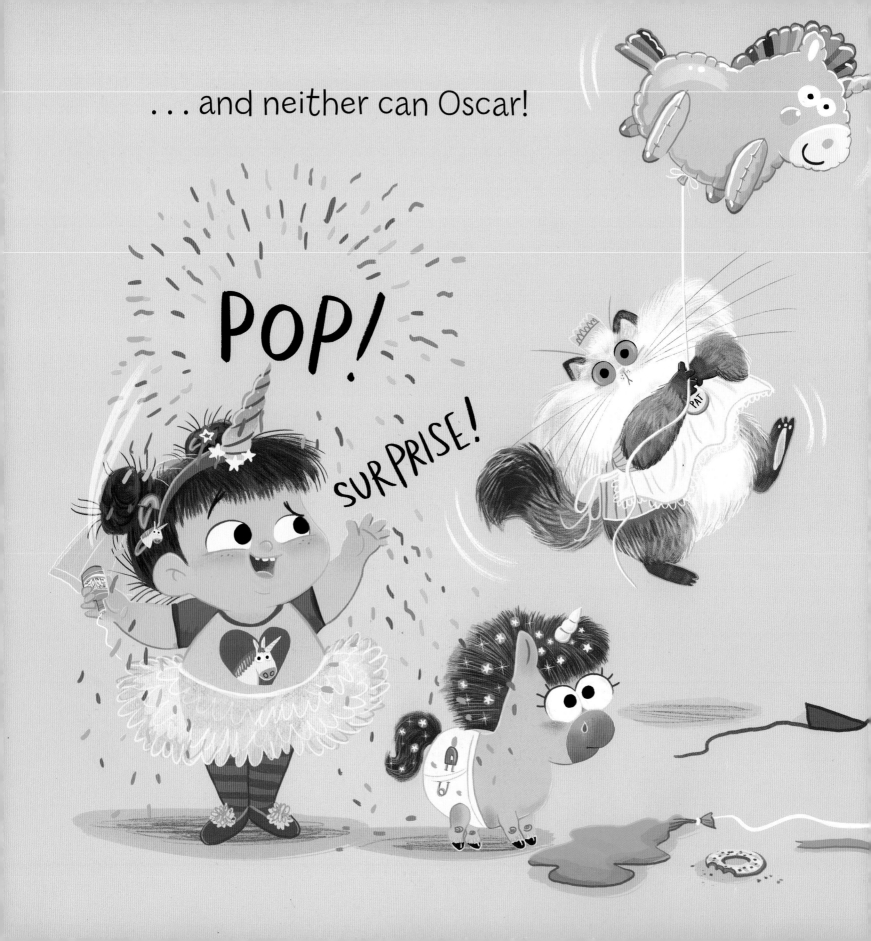

. . . and neither can Oscar!

Babycorns take a **LOT** of looking after.
Oscar will have to learn how, **AND** teach Babycorn
a thing or two about unicorning, says Oola.

PAT
PAT!

MUNCH MUNCH!

Oola shows Oscar how
to feed Babycorn.

(BUT OSCAR WOULD RATHER FEED HIMSELF.)

It's playtime now, Oola says.
(OSCAR'S TUMMY SAYS IT ISN'T.)

Oof, what a **STINK!** It must be changing time.
Oola doesn't know how they get through
nappies **SO** fast!

POOF!

(PAT THE CAT KNOWS EXACTLY HOW . . .)

It's naptime next! Oscar has a go
at rocking Babycorn to sleep.
(OSCAR MAY NOT BE CUT OUT FOR THIS BABYCORN BUSINESS.)

MEOow!!

Looking after Babycorn is the most exhausting job **EVER!**
It's Oscar's turn to be in charge while everyone else naps.
(BUT OSCAR IS BUSY AND SO IS BABYCORN.)

BABYCORN WIPES

UNI TALC

Aah, that's better. Oola has had the most
REFRESHINGEST snooze **EVER**. But wait!
Where is Babycorn?

Not here or there or ANYWHERE!

(PAT THE CAT HAS A GOOD IDEA WHERE SHE MIGHT BE.)

They **HAVE** to find her, Oola says. Even if it takes the absolute **WHOLE** night long.

But there is no sign.
Perhaps Oola's beautiful Babycorn is lost

FOREVER!

SNIFF

It must be time for a cheery-uppy
unicorn sundae, says the king.

(Oscar likes the sound of cheery-uppy unicorn sundaes.)

Oola's Babycorn was hiding all along.
Oscar is the most **wonderFULLest**
babycorn-sitter EVER, Oola says.

And Babycorn has learnt a thing or two about unicorning!